In memory of

JOHN A. T. ROBINSON

and

JOHN MCGILL KRUMM

MIRRORS OF GOD

JOSEPH W. GOETZ

Revised Edition

Originally published in 1984 by
St. Anthony Messenger Press
Cincinnati, Ohio

Illustrations by Joseph W. Goetz

ISBN 0-88028-213-4

© 1984, 1999 Joseph W. Goetz

1999, Forward Movement Publications
412 Sycamore Street, Cincinnati, Ohio 45202

CONTENTS

INTRODUCTION

SAINTS ARE TERRIBLE ROLE MODELS. Piety tends to clothe them in such unreal garments of virtue that, at best, they appear to be visitors from outer space, as charming but as alien as ET. Even the earthiest of characters undergoes this unfortunate sea-change once the process of canonization—whether formal or informal—has been embarked upon.

This is doubly unfortunate. First, because it distorts the wonderfully rich and varied truth of the Christian story, rendering it all too often into something akin to Stalinist revisions of history, thus falsifying the past. Second, but more practically and importantly, it takes out of the realm of the possible precisely what is so needed in all generations of Christians: persons who are imitable, whose life journeys can be seen to relate to the routines and adventures and opportunities of plain people like the rest of us.

Contemporary psychology amply confirms what Jesus took for granted: the need for wholesome models of behavior. When he said, "[Y]our light must shine before men that they may see goodness in your acts and give praise to your heavenly Father" (Matthew 5:15), he was acknowledging what any good teacher knows—that most of us learn by imitation. And when he condemned those who might lead "the little ones" into sin (see Matthew 18:5-7), he was almost certainly thinking of the wicked example we often give to our juniors.

One of Freud's fundamental insights concerned the measure of influence parents and significant others exert over the impressionable child. According to Freud's dictum, the pliable medium of the child's personality is sculpted into a shape resembling the final, adult image as early as three years of age. Based upon that premise, the significance of the images presented to young and old alike can hardly be overestimated. The saints obviously have little need for our adulation; we need *them* for their example.

It is this search for role models that gives rise to this book.

The six chapters of this book have grown out of six talks delivered to the Episcopal Sisters of the Transfiguration in Glendale, Ohio. The topics, chosen after extensive conversation with the sisters, turned out simply to be classic Christian themes as they apply practically to the day-to-day life of Christians living on the threshold of a new century.

I quite consciously gave each theme its Greek title to emphasize its classic status in our tradition. There is nothing newfangled about any of them. But I also wanted to link these six topics together and show how each of them is an active noun demanding engagement and work on our part. Thus:

Metanoia: converting, the daily turning to the Lord which is a continual element in the Christian life.

Koinonia: building community, not merely living gracefully within its boundaries.

Kerygma: proclaiming the Good News, allowing one's life to be an announcement of God's love.

Theologia: reasoning with all of one's faculties about the faith.

Leiturgia: worshiping the Lord in the gathered Body of Christ.

Diakonia: reaching out to others in loving service.

Other issues could have been addressed, but these six themes seemed, in the phrase beloved of old-fashioned Quakers, "to speak to our condition."

Wanting these themes or topics to take on something of the flesh and blood of real life, I chose to focus upon people, six people who seemed to me to embody, to make concrete, the virtues and qualities shrouded in those ancient Greek terms. And because I was speaking *to* women I thought it important to speak *about* women. With some significant exceptions, the examples set before Christians have too often been men. In a modest attempt to rectify that injustice, I selected six remarkable contemporary women: Dorothy Day, Anne Morrow Lindbergh, Simone Weil, Dorothy L. Sayers, Evelyn Underhill and Mother Teresa.

These six were consciously drawn from a number of religious traditions, although it was finally people and not religions which moved me to make the choices I did. Two of them are Roman Catholic, two Anglican, one nominally Presbyterian and one Jewish. I have personally met only two of them, but all have in some way, whether directly or indirectly, ministered to my faith.

These chapters are not intended to be eulogies. I have taken some pains to point out the six women's limitations and weaknesses as well as their virtues and great gifts. Akin to even the saintliest of former ages. There is an inevitable gap between what these women might have been and what they are or were.

What is certain is that these women, diverse in temperament and gifts, reveal within their very diversity the essential unity of which St. Paul wrote: "There does not exist among you Jew or Greek, slave or freeman, male or female. All are one in Christ Jesus" (Galatians 3:28).

NOTE: When this little book was first published, the ordination of women to the priesthood in the Episcopal Church was still something of a novelty. That is no longer the case, but the underlying motive for the book remains the same; sound theology not only allows for, but urges, the inclusion of women in the ordained ministry.

METANOIA:

DOROTHY DAY
AND THE DAILY
CHANGE OF HEART

DOROTHY DAY speaks for all of us when she writes in her autobiography, *The Long Loneliness:*

> Going to confession is hard—hard when you have sins to confess, hard when you haven't, and you rack your brain for even the beginnings of sins against charity, chastity, sins of detraction, sloth or gluttony. You do not want to make too much of your constant imperfections and venial sins, but you want to drag

them out to the light of day as the first step in getting rid of them. The just man falls seven times daily.

"Bless me, Father, for I have sinned," is the way you begin. "I made my last confession a week ago, and since then . . ."

Properly, one should say the *Confiteor,* but the priest has no time for that, what with the long lines of penitents on a Saturday night, so you are supposed to say it outside the confessional as you kneel in a pew, or as you stand in line with others.

"I have sinned. These are my sins." That is all you are supposed to tell; not the sins of others, or your own virtues, but only your ugly, gray, drab, monotonous sins.

GIVEN THE CHOICE to designate a saint for today, many American Catholics raised in the years before Vatican II would fix upon Dorothy Day as an embodiment of that peculiar mixture of God-centeredness and practicality appropriate to native American notions of sanctity. Memories of Roger Williams, Anne Hutchinson, Thoreau and Emerson still echo for those who think about the meaning of an *American* saintliness.

A feminist long before the ERA, an anarchist even before women had the vote, a pacifist before the Bomb, Dorothy Day moved through her long life as a kind of conscience for American

Catholics. Perhaps the reason she was able to serve in that role was her own practice of regular confession (or, as we now prefer to call it, the Sacrament of Reconciliation), which grew out of Dorothy's acute sense of sin and the need for life-long conversion.

There is something more than a little old-fashioned about Dorothy's description of making her confession—particularly now that increasing numbers have adopted the practice of face-to-face confession. I do not know what Dorothy Day's later practice was (the passage I quote is from her 1952 autobiography); but from things she mentions in her later writing, I would suspect that she preferred the old way. Not that the form matters all that much; the principal elements are always the same: humble confession, true repentance and amendment of life, absolution.

The reason for beginning with that passage is simply to remind us that her life, like that of all Christians, was one of continual conversion and not simply occasional moments of devotion. Such a reminder takes on new importance in a culture such as our own where the testimonies of born-agains to whatever is currently fashionable fill newspaper columns and air waves.

Even a superficial knowledge of Dorothy Day's pilgrimage cannot but point up for others how much the Christian life is a continuing conversion. Raised as a very nominal Christian in a middle-class family in the early years of this century (she was 81 when she died in 1980), it was not until her late 20's that she began to feel called to something more than the life she had been living, that of a vaguely bohemian, socially conscious feminist. The first of her many jail terms resulted from agitating about the imprisonment of suffragists in the years just prior to World War I. By her 30th year, having borne a daughter out of wedlock to the man with whom she had entered a common-law relationship, she "found herself," as she quite literally believed, by entering the Roman Catholic Church.

Her subsequent career—the friendship with Peter Maurin which led her to found with him the first of many houses for the derelict and the destitute; the establishment of *The Catholic Worker* as a continuing voice of Christian social dissent from the all-too-easy accommodation of most Christians to war and poverty and prejudice; her willingness to go to prison for her stands against nuclear preparedness, racism and indeed the oppression of prisoners themselves—all is well documented in her own and others' books. Someone once said that Dorothy's vocation was to comfort the afflicted increasingly and to afflict the comfortable unceasingly.

Colman McCarthy remarked in the *New*

Republic that Dorothy Day had "the wild extreme notion that Christianity is a workable system, the bizarre idea that religion has more to do with what you work at than what you believe." I suspect Dorothy Day's response to that would have been to say that it matters enormously what you believe, for it is out of faith—or the lack thereof—that you do what you do.

And it was her faith and the continuing conversion that was her life which makes her memory green for many, partly because her experience was not so different from that of each of us. She believed in the face of a good deal of evidence to the contrary that every human being is a child of God and, therefore, demands the respect and care and love due to a son or daughter of the King. When an elderly woman prisoner in a West Virginia prison queried "Why are you here?" Dorothy is supposed to have responded with the simple and honest words, "We have come to wash your feet." That sums up very well indeed what she was to many of us less committed, more half-hearted Christians.

I HAVE USED OF HER, and of ourselves, the phrase *conversion of life*. By this I mean that the event of *metanoia*, conversion, starts a lifelong process going, although for some of us the event itself may be sudden and utterly unpredicted. The gospel is, of course, bad news before it is good news. The *bad* news is that we are sinners in need of conversion. But in the end it is *good* news: God forgives us.

The real beginning of the lifetime process of conversion is *not* the acknowledgment of our sins. That is common to all of us, atheists and believers alike; we all know what miserable rotters we are. Conversion begins rather with the acceptance of God's forgiveness, the conviction that the gospel is good news and not just a piece of grim information we know already if we are honest. It is the acceptance of God's forgiveness which sets in motion this lifelong business of *metanoia*, of turning everything upside down and saying that to gain one's life one must lose it, that the servant is the master, that the first is last and the last is first, that the poor are rich and the rich shall be sent away empty, that we are all here to wash one another's feet.

That is very hard for most of us to accept. Something in us makes us suspect that God's forgiveness is too good to be true. Therefore we struggle against it, or water it down, or turn it into something it is not meant to be, at least not initially: a program of self-improvement.

Many of us have a deep-seated need to feel guilty. That is perhaps why it is sometimes so difficult to accept God's forgiveness. Psychologists can give us reasons why some human beings find it so important to feel guilt. But as St. Augustine writes in his *Confessions*, there is something in each of us which even our own spirits do not know. We may leave it at that.

The acceptance of God's forgiveness leaves us vulnerable. As we acknowledge our need for forgiveness, not just for all that is past but for all that will be, so we admit that—at least in this life—we shall never be anything but forgiven sinners, *justus simul et peccator.* In reading Dorothy Day's writings, one becomes aware that this is precisely how she described herself. In a period in which many devote themselves to an almost obsessive concern with self-actualization (Christopher Lasch calls it "the culture of narcissism"), there is something bracing about a person who is prepared to acknowledge that, at her best, she is a "forgiven sinner."

FOR A RATHER SMALL NUMBER of people conversion is an extraordinary, almost catastrophic, act in which everything is turned topsy-turvy, after which nothing is ever again the same. The most obvious examples are Paul, the persecutor turned apostle; Francis, the debonair young courtier become poor man; Martin Luther, a sin-obsessed monk transformed into a radical reformer. But for most of us, as for Dorothy, conversion is a lifelong process. She always spoke of herself as "on pilgrimage."

Paul Tillich once very reluctantly answered the question as to whether he was a Christian by replying, "Every morning I must pray that I shall *become* a Christian." It is indeed a process of becoming, not an achieved state of being. This facet of the Christian life has been beautifully expressed by the South African poet Alan Paton in his "Meditation for a Young Boy Confirmed":

> This kneeling, this signing, this reading from ancient books,
> This acknowledgment that the burden is intolerable, this promise of amendment,
> This humble access, this putting out of the hands,
> This taking of the bread and wine, this return to your place not glancing about you,
> This solemn acceptance and the thousand sins that will follow it, this thousand sins and the repenting of them,
> This dedication and this apostasy, this apostasy and this restoration,
> This thousand restorations and this thousand apostasies,
> Take and accept them all, be not affronted nor dismayed by them.
> They are a net of holes to capture essence, a shell to house the thunder of an ocean,

A discipline of petty acts to catch Creation, a
    rune of words to hold One Living Word,
A Ladder built by men of sticks and stones,
    whereby they hope to reach to heaven.

Spiritual writers call this painful struggle "a dying to self," a concept based on the Pauline notion that Christians always "carry about in our bodies the dying of Jesus, so that in our bodies the life of Jesus may also be revealed" (2 Corinthians 4:10). Each day, then, this dying to self (or, more positively, this becoming the real self) demands a continual conversion. The self to which we die may be a proud, grasping, ambitious, self-centered egoist, or it may be a guilt-ridden, self-loathing, self-rejecting egoist. Whichever, die to it we must.

Reduced to its simplest dimensions, this day-in, day-out conversion is a renewal of one's humble acceptance of God's forgiveness. An Anglican bishop, Dr. Peter Walker, put it beautifully in his enthronement sermon in the great Cathedral Church at Ely in East Anglia. He described how he and his wife had been on a brief holiday in Tuscany and had been urged by friends to stop and see a quite remarkable 15th-century church with some paintings by one of the Bellinis. As they walked up the nave of the church, the bishop reported, his eyes were drawn to a piece of brown wrapping paper pinned to the front of the pulpit. On it were written the words *Ora, Dio ti ama!* ("God loves you now!").

It is precisely this awareness, humbly appropriated into one's own life, that is the foundation stone of the conversion process. If we truly believe that God loves us *now* for what we are *now,* no strings attached, then we cannot but be embarked on that conversion of heart and manners which is the essence of the response to the invitation of Jesus. Those of us who heard the Bishop of Ely on that autumn day were grateful to him for refocusing for us, in the midst of a ceremonial of great splendor and pomp, the utter simplicity of the Christian message: God loves you now!

THE SACRAMENT of Reconciliation (Confession) should be seen in the light of this continuing process of conversion of life. One person may prefer the older and more traditional way of receiving it: kneeling at the prie-dieu and behind a screen, confessing sins, promising true amendment of life and receiving the Church's absolution; and that is perfectly suitable if that is what the individual prefers. Others are happy to use a less structured form of auricular confession, seated and face-to-face with the confessor, receiving the sacrament within the context of a natural and prayerful conversation. Many younger people prefer to receive the sacrament in this way, partly because of bad past associations in which it was felt that the priest was merely perfunctory in his ministry, party because the anonymous approach tended to take the form of a kind of "laundry list" of sins rattled off more or less unintelligibly.

Whichever way we prefer to get "scraped" (to use the phrase beloved of English Roman Catholic prep-school boys), scraped we need to be! And this practice needs to be seen as a sign of continuing conversion. Christians who regularly make use of this sacrament will want to guard against the deadening effect of routine—for which reason the sacrament must never be taken for granted. Dorothy Day once said that the best way to receive the Sacrament of Penance is to suppose that it will be—as one day it must—the *last* confession.

A life in which the process of conversion is consciously and gratefully acknowledged will be a life alerted to what Paul calls "newness of life." In Romans 6:4 he writes, "Through baptism into his death we were buried with him, so that, just as Christ was raised from the dead by the glory of the Father, we too might live a new life."

Sometimes the awareness of life's newness is so vivid as to be sensually experienced: like a warm spring day after months of bitter winter cold, or a heavy burden lifted from the shoulders.

And then the heart leaps up for the sheer joy of it. More often, of course, we continue the plodding path most of us follow, trying to translate into the distinctive dialect of our own individual lives the message that God forgives us, that in and by Jesus we are truly reconciled to the Father.

For Dorothy Day that daily conversion of life meant an extraordinary pilgrimage with long stints in jail for her pacifism and other unpopular beliefs, as well as the never-ending routine of daily service to God's poor in houses of hospitality across the country. For each of us that daily conversion of life will mean different things: doing what we are called by God to do or, rather, *being* what we are called by God to *be*—kinder, more sensitive to the needs of others (or of oneself), more restrained in the use of one's appetites, more hopeful and honest. But it all begins in the same place, with the incredible news that God so loves us that he forgives us anything. That piece of news should—if we really believed it—have the effect of turning us upside down and inside out.

If—and what an enormous "if" that is—we really believe that God loves us *now,* everything undergoes a *metanoia,* everything looks different than it does by the light of common day. Let me give you an example.

I have a colleague whom I take for granted

or, more accurately, whom I find very hard to take at all. But if God loves him now, there is something—perhaps the "something" St. Augustine was referring to, about which even my colleague may not consciously know—which makes him utterly lovable in God's sight. Similarly with the stranger who suddenly and inconveniently stumbles into my life: God loves that person *now*. Can I do any less?

The world around me, the gray wintry day when nothing goes as I had hoped, with burnt breakfast and tardy appointments, with tiresome phone calls and a stuck desk drawer, with all that Virgil calls "the tears in things" making themselves felt: "Yes!" I say to myself, "but God loves me now!" And suddenly the dross of that routine is converted by the alchemy of divine love into a treasure "wondrous fair and passing strange." Everything—bores and strangers and leaden days, even ourselves—can be converted from base metal into the gold of God's love. Dorothy Day seems to have been one of those Christians for whom this conversion of the routine and the ugly and the despairing was a daily event. Would that it could be so for all of us!

Christians might give thought to saying over and over again, "God loves me now!" Said often enough, there may be a miraculous moment in which its truth strikes home and suddenly one hears oneself saying, "Yes, it is true! God loves me now." Then the lifetime of conversion will really begin.

Anne Morrow Lindbergh
and Building
the Earth

THERE IS AN OBVIOUS COROLLARY to the conviction that "God loves you now." If that statement is hard to appropriate into one's life, its complement is even harder: "God loves *all* people now." The difficulty in accepting that second assertion is that the "people" God loves are not "people in general," but the quite specific individuals with whom one's life is somehow linked. The basis for that conviction is that all human beings are surrounded by God's love and are therefore a community of love. The fundamental relationship in the Christian faith is not "me and Jesus"; it is "we and Jesus," a concept ultimately based on the New Testament notion of *koinonia,* the Greek word for "community."

The life of Anne Morrow Lindbergh has been one of intense struggle between a deeply shy and introspective personality and the public responsibility—even celebrity—forced upon her by circumstance. But the widow of the American aviator Charles Lindbergh, herself a pioneer flier and a gifted poet and writer, has learned the art of living gracefully in the human community while committing herself to its upbuilding. Her life and her writings reveal her sense of being part of a much larger community than most of us can conceive.

In 1938 Anne Morrow Lindbergh and her husband were living with their two children in Paris. It was a time of grave international anxiety, for the wheels leading to the horrors of World War II were turning inexorably. And the tension reflected in the newspapers, with one barely averted crisis after another ("Chamberlain Flies to Munich" was the almost weekly headline), was translated into the smaller but no less worrying anxieties of ordinary life.

In a diary entry for Friday, November 25, 1938, Anne Lindbergh described the sculptor, Charles Despiau, who was engaged in doing her head:

> He says he is always afraid when he starts a new piece of work. Nothing he has done before gives him any confidence. He is afraid as though it were the first piece of work he had ever done. He is not afraid of death at all and tells me of a narrow escape he once had driving horses in the snow. But he says he is afraid of himself, of traveling, of new places, sometimes even of going to the tobacco store to get some cigarettes.
>
> I understand it well. It would be easy to get like that and I have tendencies that way as it is.
>
> *(The Flower and the Nettle)*

In this revealing passage Anne Lindbergh discloses a good deal about herself and her extraordinarily paradoxical life. It is in the context of that life of paradox that we may be led to learn more about the nature of Christian community.

In the diaries* and letters Anne wrote before

---

*Five volumes of her diaries have been published: *Bring Me a Unicorn*, 1922-1928; *Hour of Gold, Hour of Lead*, 1929-1932; *Locked Rooms and Open Doors*, 1932-1935; *The Flower and the Nettle*, 1936-1939; and *War Within, War Without*, 1940-1944.

she met Lindbergh, one encounters a profoundly lonely girl, surrounded by the mercurial affection of eccentric but highly gifted parents and of her sisters and brother. She describes herself in the slang of that period as a "wallflower," never asked to dance, always on the outskirts of events. The agony and uncertainty that attends all of us when we are first introduced into adult company seems to have stayed with her a much longer time, heightened of course by the appalling glare of publicity in which much of her young married life had to be lived.

The miracle is that she managed with grace and wit and compassion to break out of the stranglehold of introspection and almost self-imposed isolation. By her writings she has held up a mirror to the world which allows all of us to see in it something of our true image, a community of human beings whose lives are woven together in a sometimes simple, sometimes exceedingly complex pattern of dependency and mutual responsibility.

She was brought up in an upper-class home. Her father, a self-made millionaire banker, was described by his partner, J. P. Morgan, as a man so selfish that he would have murdered his own children if they had stood in his way. Her mother was a vigorous, rather exhausting person given to sudden enthusiasms and "doing good."

Educated conventionally but well, Anne's experience was broadened by travel and an almost constant stream of powerful and influential visitors through her parents' house in Englewood, New Jersey.

Anne Morrow, nonetheless, was an insecure and, from her own description, rather gauche debutante when she first met America's hero, Charles Lindbergh, at the Mexican Embassy in 1928. As it gradually dawned that Colonel Lindbergh's affection for the Morrow family was more than merely diplomatic, Anne immediately assumed that it was her sister Elizabeth who had attracted the attention of the "Lone Eagle," since she saw herself as too plain and dull to be of interest to so exciting a man.

She describes, under the phrase "hour of gold," the excitement and adventure of the early years of their marriage, their first flights together, the gaiety with which they eluded the bloodhound-like surveillance of the press. It was for them a time culminating in the birth of their first child, a son.

The unspeakable tragedy of their child's kidnapping and murder in 1932 served only to reinforce her own desperate need for privacy and a quiet life. Escaping to Europe in 1935, she and her husband forged the semblance of a normal life for themselves and their growing family until forced to return to the United States on the eve of World War II.

ONE OF THE PEOPLE the Lindberghs encountered in Europe during those prewar years, through their mutual friends Dr. Alexis Carrel and his wife, was the Jesuit paleontologist, Pierre Teilhard de Chardin. After meeting him Anne wrote: ". . . I felt better for knowing his mind is in the world."

After World War II and continuing beyond her husband's death in 1979, Anne Lindbergh, through her writings and the projects she has supported (environmentalism, for example), has witnessed to an image of what the world should be and seldom is: a community bound together by mutual concern and affection.

Anne Lindbergh herself admits that her sensitivity to the earth as a whole, as a planet, is the result of her experience as an aviator. In her book *Earth Shine* she writes:

> Looking down from above, they could discern more clearly the bones of earth and were aware, as Saint-Exupery was, of how ephemeral is the flesh that clothes it—that fragile flower of life, growing on its surface, "like a little moss in the crevices."

But if it is true that fliers—especially those early pioneers—thought and felt terrestrially, it took someone like Père Teilhard to put that awareness into words. As he said of himself, he wanted "to express the psychology—the mixed feelings of pride, hope, disappointment, expectation—of the man who sees himself no longer as a Frenchman or a Chinaman but as a Terrestrial." In her diary Anne Lindbergh quotes the American poet, Abie Huston Evans, and makes the sentiments her own:

> The terrible whorl of the Milky Way shines
> out
> To newt-eyes under; glory bears down ton-
> like;
> Ordeal girdles us in. I marvel we live.
> Yet live we do in the maelstrom, mites as we
> are;
> On our acorn shook from the Oak, we ride out
> the dark.

What Mrs. Lindbergh called her "terrestrial consciousness" is expressed in a complementary way by the molecular biologist Lewis Thomas in his Pulitzer Prize-winning book, *The Lives of a Cell:*

> *Item.* The *uniformity* of the earth's life, more astonishing than its diversity, is accountable by the high probability that we derived,

originally, from some single cell, fertilized in the bolt of lightning as the earth cooled. It is from the progeny of this parent cell that we take our looks; we still share genes around, and the resemblance of the enzymes of grasses to those of whales is a family resemblance.

These differing and yet complementary ways of looking at interrelatedness are linked by a common perception: Somehow we are parts of a greater whole, genetically, geographically, terrestrially, even cosmically. The underlying conviction is that there *is* a pattern, an order, however much of the detail we are bound to miss because our eyes are too blind or our minds too finite.

I need to remind myself of that often because it lends a sympathy, a compassion, a deepening of my understanding—not only of my fellow human beings but of the good earth itself and of the shining stars. Anne Lindbergh's experience as a flier and her sensitivity as a poet help confirm for me the deep truth that we are all part of each other—which is to say, in the language of the New Testament, we are the Body of Christ.

There is more to be said, of course. We are not only parts of the whole but each of us is utterly unique, like a snowflake or the dance of electrons in an atom. And that uniqueness needs to be lifted up, celebrated and renewed. In her book *Gift From the Sea*, Mrs. Lindbergh reflects the paradox so hard for many of us to learn: A gift for belonging to others, taking responsibility for them, allowing them to take responsibility for ourselves, demands times of replenishment, of solitude. As Dietrich Bonhoffer said, "The person who cannot be alone had better be afraid to be with others."

Anne Lindbergh develops this theme meditating on a moon shell found while spending a few days alone on the beach:

Moon shell, who named you? Some intuitive woman I like to think. I shall give you another name—Island Shell. I cannot live forever on my island. But I can take you back to my desk in Connecticut. You will sit there and fasten your single eye on me. You will make me think, with your smooth circles winding inward to the tiny core, of the island I lived on for a few weeks. You will say to me "solitude." You will remind me that I must try to be alone for part of each year, even a week or a few days; and for part of each day, even for an hour or for a few minutes in order to keep my core, my center, my island-quality. You will remind me that unless I keep the island-quality intact somewhere within me, I will have little to give my husband, my children, my friends or the world at large. You will remind me that woman must be still as the axis of a wheel in the midst of her activities; that she must be the pioneer in achieving this stillness, not only for her own salvation, but for the salvation of family life, of society, perhaps even of our civilization.

(Gift From the Sea)

To be a responsible and responsive member of a community, whether it be the so-called nuclear family or a great and powerful nation, each of us needs to find time apart for silence, for solitude, for meditation. I used to tell my students that for a priest to be engaged in a whirlwind of activity and good works without a corresponding period of silence and solitude is to court what Bishop Michael Ramsey once called "one-dimensionality," that is, a superficially energetic ministry without depth and, ultimately, with nothing to give worth giving. The Gospel of Mark records for us Jesus' words to his disciples after the heady experience of their first missionary journeys:

> The apostles returned to Jesus and reported to him all they had done and what they had taught. He said to them: "Come by yourselves to an out-of-the-way place and rest a while." People were coming and going in great numbers, making it impossible for them to so much as eat. (Mark 6:30-31)

One suspects the disciples' response, although it's not recorded, was something like, "Look, Lord, the time is ripe. We haven't the luxury to get away from it all!" The truth the Lord was urging upon them was that such moments are needed to revitalize our involvement in and commitment to the wider community of which we are a part. What is needed is a "critical distance" from the usual responsibilities and challenges and difficulties of community membership. It is for the sake of a deeper commitment to our community engagement that we need such time alone.

THE NECESSITY of occasional retreat from community engagement may be the caution many of us need to hear. But others of us can just as easily identify with Anne Lindbergh in her honest self-appraisal that, were she to depend entirely on her own wishes and tastes, she would lead a very circumscribed life, open only to the few, isolated from the many. When some community activity presents itself (voting in the November election, attending a committee meeting, helping a beggar in the street), we know the persistent voice of temptation that whispers in our ear: "You won't be missed."

But if St. Paul is right, then you will be missed:

The body is one and has many members, but all the members, many though they are, are one body; and so it is with Christ. It was in one Spirit that all of us, whether Jew or Greek, slave or free, were baptized into one body. All of us have been given to drink of the one Spirit. (1 Corinthians 12:12-13)

Even if one is not daily engaged in a nuclear family or a religious community, it is still important to know how to invest oneself in community building, as contemporary jargon will have it. "Community building" may have a slightly new ring to it but it is nothing other than insuring that each of us reflects the old virtues of forbearance and kindness and compassion in our life together. There are no shortcuts to living peacefully and creatively together.

Anne Morrow Lindbergh urges upon us the aviator's eye with which to discern how closely linked we are to each other. Lewis Thomas suggests that we think of ourselves as inheritors with all living creatures of a genetic heritage which makes us sharers in the mystery of creation. Teilhard de Chardin described in *The Divine Milieu* the mystical affinity he felt as a young boy to a rock that he had picked up quite at random: Its *haeceitas*, its "thisness," as the medievals called the uniqueness of individuality, triggered in him a sense of creatureliness, of humility in the face of creation, which he never forgot.

But all of these serve to confirm what Paul, clearly in continuity with the teaching of Jesus, articulated about our membership in a Body far larger than the eye can see or even the mind can stretch. It was of course Jesus himself who broke through the barrier of religious and racial isolation when he reached out to those in need, regardless of the purity of their belief or the regularity of their lives. If it is true that every person is my neighbor (however distant or alien or unknown to me), then we are brothers and sisters in that larger fellowship which no one can count, a community without boundaries.

Anne Lindbergh echoes the Christian tradition when, in her writings, she suggests that the clue to living together (with husband and children, with other vowed persons, with a parish "family" of 1,300 households, with whatever community we find ourselves part of, temporarily or permanently) is simply love. And she emphasizes the need to respect the uniqueness, the integrity of the others with whom one has entered into a community relationship—an emphasis which echoes St. Paul:

> Love is patient; love is kind. Love is not jealous, it does not put on airs, it is not snobbish.

Love is never rude, it is not self-seeking, it is
not prone to anger; neither does it brood over
injuries. Love does not rejoice in what is wrong
but rejoices with the truth. There is no limit to
love's forbearance, to its trust, its hope, its
power to endure. (1 Corinthians 13:4-7)

TO LIVE IN A COMMUNITY is to live a fully
personal relationship. Anne Lindbergh makes her
own the description of such a relationship given
by the Scottish philosopher John Macmurray, who
emphasized that so to live demands the whole of
ourselves.

Personal relationships have no ulterior motive.
They are not based on particular interests.
They do not serve partial ends. Their value
lies entirely in themselves and for the same
reason transcends all other values. And that
is because they are relations of persons as
persons.

"Persons as persons": How easy it is for us to
fall into a pattern in which we regard others as
means to an end or as obstacles to that end! To be
part of a community of personal relationships is
to forswear the traditional patterns of domina-
tion and submission, possession and competition.
The *koinonia*-Christian is one who allows space
and freedom for growth in solidarity with

others. Anne Lindbergh quotes the German poet Rilke's description of community:

> a relation that is meant to be of one human to another . . . And this more human love . . . will resemble that which we are—with struggle and endeavor—preparing, the love that consists in this, that two solitudes protect and touch each other.

Rilke's phrase "two solitudes" highlights yet another aspect of community. For there is a sense in which every community, however large or small, consists of "solitudes." It is never possible for any of us to pass completely beyond the barrier of our own individuality into the virtually undiscovered country of the other's individuality. But living in a community of love means that we honor the other's uniqueness, even as we hope that our own individuality will be respected. As we are separate, so we are joined—by so much more than is on the surface and merely visible.

"Looking from a plane," Anne Lindbergh once remarked, "makes me feel closer to the earth and everyone on it than many days in a teeming city." She expressed as well as any contemporary writer our kinship, our uniqueness, our interrelatedness, our dependency. True enough, she would say, we need solitude, but only to give more to those with whom we live. We rejoice in our uniqueness, but only so as to celebrate more authentically the gifts each has to bring to the common banquet of life.

"God loves me now" is complemented by a very similar assertion, "God loves you now." But perfection is achieved when we say, "God loves us now!"

KERYGMA:

SIMONE WEIL
AND PROCLAIMING THE CROSS

CHRISTIANS ARE CALLED to be heralds, proclaimers of the gospel. What can be said of one who, though unable to bring herself to accept Christian Baptism because of the historical circumstances in which she lived, nonetheless assumed that same responsibility of proclamation? Simone Weil, regarded by T. S. Eliot as one of the "saints" in an unsaintly age, remains an enigma and yet serves to remind contemporary Christians that all of us are heralds.

"God loves you now" the scrap of brown paper declared to all who looked at that pulpit in a Tuscan church. Not only is it important for us to believe that this is so, but it must be proclaimed. Putting it very simply, somebody had to go to the trouble of writing that phrase down and then tacking it up so people could see it. Just as we need to hear the Good News, so there must be some among us who proclaim it. Someone must be a *keryx*, a herald, to announce the message, the *kerygma*. The third of our six women is precisely such a herald.

SIMONE WEIL was an extremely complex person. Exasperating in the extreme and yet utterly interesting, she was not at all the boring paragon some would make her into. She once wrote to a friend, "Everything interests me," and this was so. Her brilliant and original mind romped from philosophy to poetry to literary criticism to political sociology. Nothing was exempt from the sustained and ruthlessly honest gaze she fixed upon the world into which she was born. She was, as not a few geniuses turn out to be, hypersensitive and generous to a fault—the sort of person who goes to any extreme to be of use and ends by inconveniencing everyone.

She had a particular sensitivity to outcasts. One of her friends remarked that, had Simone stayed in New York in 1942, "she would surely have become a Negress," meaning that Simone Weil had an unerring eye for the downtrodden and the oppressed, with whom she wished sincerely to cast her lot.

T.S. Eliot, in the preface to the 1949 edition of the posthumously published work, *The Need for Roots,* said of her that she lived her life "with a genius akin to that of the saints." From about 1935 until her death in 1943 Simone Weil seems to have lived a life of high mystical prayer; and it is perhaps for this that she is now best remembered. Her life was too short for all of her gifts to have come to full flower, but she remains one or the most enigmatic and fascinating characters in the intellectual history of our century.

The outline of her brief but remarkable life suggests something of the enigma which she remains. She was born in 1909 to secularized Jewish parents in Paris. From early on she showed high promise in her philosophical studies and received in quick succession the higher degrees necessary for fulfilling her initial hope: a career in teaching. Even in her teens she showed a sympathy for Marxism, pacifism, the trade union movement and, most especially, for the working classes. She so wished to be identified with the latter that for about a year, until her health would not permit it, she worked as a factory hand.

In 1937, even though she still professed pacifism, she went to the front during the Spanish Civil War. (Typically, she managed to survive bombs and machine guns but succeeded in burning herself with cooking oil so badly that she had to be sent home.) As war became more and more inevitably the end result of the belligerence of the European powers, Simone Weil's health deteriorated. She nonetheless managed to draw up a memorandum for a front-line nursing squad which would be a French counterpoint to Hitler's superbly trained Storm Troopers. The nurses would be unarmed, willing to go into the worst areas of battle to tend the wounded immediately, and would serve to focus world public opinion upon the triumph of right over might. This praiseworthy but wholly impractical scheme was finally shelved by the French government.

As it became more and more obvious that the Nazi occupation of France would endanger the lives of even French Jews, Simone Weil and her parents fled first to Vichy, then to North Africa and finally, in 1942, to the United States.

During this American period Simone Weil was engaged in the most intense mystical contemplation. She attended daily Mass at the Church of Corpus Christi near Columbia University. (Since this was also the parish to which

Thomas Merton belonged, it is interesting to speculate that, at least for a time, two of the most influential spiritual writers in our century may have been sitting in the same pew without knowing one another.)

But Simone Weil was impatient to return to Europe to lend her own enormous talents to the war effort, having shed her pacifism when Hitler invaded Czechoslovakia. She finally reached England in late 1942 and was given a post with the French resistance in London. Her never very robust health continued to afflict her, a condition aggravated by the fact that she frequently refused to eat because people in occupied France were dying of hunger. She continued to turn away medical treatment and nourishment until she finally died in August of 1943 of starvation and pulmonary tuberculosis. (Some contemporary commentators suggest that her real illness was *anorexia nervosa*.)

IN T. S. ELIOT'S 1949 PLAY *The Cocktail Party,* the character of Celia Coplestone (a young woman whose life suddenly ends while she is serving as a member of an austere nursing order in a missionary station in Africa) seems to have been based, at least partly, upon Simone Weil. At one point, while Celia is attempting to discern the sort of life to which she is called, she says something to her psychiatrist which gives us a clue to the life of Simone Weil:

But even if I find my way out of the forest
I shall be left with the inconsolable memory
Of the treasure I went into the forest to find
And never found, and which was not there
And perhaps is not anywhere? But if not
    anywhere,
Why do I feel guilty at not having found it?

Nothing again can either hurt or heal.
I have thought at moments that the ecstasy is
    real
Although those who experience it may have
    no reality.
For what happened is remembered like a
    dream
In which one is exalted by intensity of loving
In the spirit, a vibration of delight
Without desire, for desire is fulfilled
In the delight of loving. A state one does not
    know
When awake. But what or whom I loved,
Or what in me was loving, I do not know.
And if that is all meaningless, I want to be
    cured
Of a craving for something I cannot find
And of the shame of never finding it.

Simone Weil's pilgrimage, brief as it was, was an attempt to discover the identity of that one whom she knew she loved and who loved her. She desired not only to identify him for herself but to call him to the attention of others. At Easter, 1938, while the migraine headaches which had compelled her to stop teaching were still in their acutest phase, she went with her mother to Solesmes to hear the Gregorian chant at the services. She succeeded in attending to the music in spite of her pain.

> An extreme effort of attention enabled me to get outside this miserable flesh, leaving it to suffer by itself, heaped up in its corner, and to find a pure and perfect joy in the unspeakable beauty of the chanting and the words. This experience enabled me by analogy to understand better the possibility of loving the divine love in the midst of affliction.

Eliot's Celia Coplestone found, according to the play, that her vocation was to minister to plague-stricken natives in Kinkanja, there to endure a seemingly meaningless death at the superstitious hands of those she had come to serve. Simone Weil's call involved a very similar witness to the Cross, "divine love in the midst of affliction."

BUT WHY PLACE SIMONE WEIL under the rubic or category of *kerygma*, proclamation? She was by any usual standards a very strange sort of evangelist. What did she proclaim by her writings and, perhaps more importantly, by her life which makes such classification possible?

In important ways her ministry was similar to that of another uprooted Jew who wrote:

> Since in God's wisdom the world did not come to know him through "wisdom," it pleased God to save those who believe through the absurdity of the preaching of the gospel. Yes, Jews demand "signs" and Greeks look for "wisdom," but we preach Christ crucified—a stumbling block to Jews, and an absurdity to Gentiles; but to those who are called, Jews and Greeks alike, Christ the power of God and the wisdom of God. For God's folly is wiser than men, and his weakness more powerful than men. (1 Corinthians 1:21-25)

Simone Weil proclaimed the foolishness of God, which is to say, she proclaimed the Cross.

Living as she did in a time when millions knew indescribable suffering and being acutely sensitive to the suffering of others, there was a certain logic in her emphasis upon the Cross. But we would seriously misunderstand her message if we supposed it to be only an accident of history. Her deepest conviction was that the Cross is the central reality at all times and in all places.

She seems to have discerned the Cross as a theme interwoven through the reality of joy and affliction—what some theologians have treated under the concept of *kenosis*. This Greek word is used in the Christological hymn in Philippians to describe the Son's humbling of himself, which is translated as "emptied himself":

Your attitude must be that of Christ:

> Though he was in the form of God,
>   he did not deem equality with
>   God something to be grasped at.

> Rather, he emptied himself
>   and took the form of a slave,
>   being born in the likeness of men.
>   (Philippians 2:5-7)

This concept of *kenosis,* self-emptying, has important implications for the Christian life. Some theologians argue that the *kenosis* of Jesus is somehow a mirroring of the *kenosis* of the Godhead; thus, a like measure of *kenosis*, self-emptying, must be found in anyone who follows Jesus.

In the story of the human Jesus who humbled himself and was obedient to death, even death on a cross, we encounter self-emptying to a degree we believe to be unique in human history. And in this man who manifests the depth of true humanity we see a glory or—and this is the same thing differently expressed—we are confronted with an ultimate claim.

This glory and this ultimacy evoke God-language—the only language adequate to express something of what has come to light in him. When we use God-language in speaking of Jesus, we mean that the self-emptying (or, to use Simone Weil's term, "the affliction") of Jesus Christ not only reveals the depth of true humanity; it also reveals that the final reality, divinity itself, is likewise self-emptying, self-giving, self-limiting—in some mysterious way "afflicted." Simone Weil expressed it this way in her essay "The Love of God and Affliction":

> The Trinity and the Cross are the two poles of Christianity, the two essential truths: the first, perfect joy; the second, perfect affliction. It is necessary to know both the one and the other and their mysterious unity, but the human condition in this world places us infinitely far from the Trinity, at the very foot of the Cross. Our country is the Cross.
>
> (*The Simone Weil Reader*)

The "mysterious unity" which links the Trinity and the Cross makes it possible to say that

God's country, too, is the Cross. The kenosis implied in the Incarnation can be interpreted as only a moment—though indeed the climactic one—in a whole history of divine kenosis.

Creation itself is kenosis. God, as it were, limits himself by sharing the gift of existence with his creatures. It is by this self-giving that God shows himself to be God and enables us to see the mysterious link between *kenosis*, "self-emptying," and *plerosis*, "fullness of being." By pouring himself out in creation, God evokes our worship, for he identifies himself with our human condition, even our affliction, and manifests his creative and redemptive love. God too knows the reality of the Cross.

As George Herbert put it in his poem "Redemption":

Having been tenant long to a rich Lord,
    Not thriving, I resolved to be bold,
    And make a suit unto him, to afford
A new small-rental lease, and cancel the old.

In heaven at his manor I him sought;
    They told me there that he was lately gone
    About some land, which he had dearly
        bought
Long since on earth, to take possession.

I straight returned, and knowing his great
    birth,

Sought him accordingly in great resorts;
In cities, theaters, gardens, parks, and
 courts;

At length I heard a ragged noise and mirth
 Of thieves and murderers; there I him
  espied,
 Who straight, *your suit is granted,* said, and
  died.

HEALTHY, WELL-ADJUSTED PEOPLE shrink
from the reality of the Cross. but Simone Weil
argues that, since the Cross is mysteriously
related not only to Jesus but to God, the fundamental reality of all existence, then so must it be
with us. However much we prefer to reduce
Christianity to cheerfulness and positive thinking, to speak of Jesus, to speak of God, to speak
of Reality itself is to speak of the Cross. As she
says:

 If we dispose our thoughts in this way, then
 after a certain time the Cross of Christ should
 become the very substance of our life. No
 doubt that is what Christ meant when he
 advised his friends to bear their cross each day,
 and not, as people seem to think nowadays,
 simply that one should be resigned about
 one's little daily troubles—which, by an
 almost sacrilegious abuse of language, people

sometimes refer to as crosses. There is only one cross; it is the whole of that necessity by which the infinity of space and time is filled and which, in given circumstances, can be concentrated upon the atom that any one of us is, and totally pulverize it.

But why should this be so? It is that little word *why* which runs like a leitmotif through this terrible century: *Why* this terrible suffering? Simone Weil suggests that it is not the affliction of other people, except sometimes those very close to us, which provokes this question. It is when we fall into affliction that the question takes hold and goes on repeating itself incessantly. Christ himself asked it: "Why has thou forsaken me?"

But, says Simone Weil, there can be no answer to the *why* of the afflicted except for *silence*. Silence *is* the answer. As she explains:

He who is capable not only of listening but also of loving hears this silence as the word of God.

The speech of created beings is with sounds. The word of God is silence. God's secret word of love can be nothing else but silence. Christ is the silence of God.

Just as there is no tree like the Cross, so there is no harmony like the silence of God. The Pythagoreans discerned this harmony in

47

the fathomless eternal silence around the stars. In this world, necessity is the vibration of God's silence.

Our soul is constantly clamorous with noise, but there is one point in it which is silence, and which we never hear. When the silence of God comes to the soul and penetrates it and joins the silence which is secretly in us, from then on we have our treasure and our heart in God; and space opens before us as the opening fruit of a plant divides in two, for we are seeing the universe from a point situated outside space.

This operation can take place in only two ways, to the exclusion of all others. There are only two things piercing enough to penetrate our souls in this way; they are affliction and beauty.

Often, one could weep tears of blood to think how many unfortunates are crushed by affliction without knowing how to make use of it. But, cooly considered, this is not a more pitiful waste than the squandering of the world's beauty. The brightness of stars, the sound of sea-waves, the silence of the hour before dawn—how often do they not offer themselves in vain to men's attention? To pay no attention to the world's beauty is, perhaps, so great a crime of ingratitude that it deserves the punishment of affliction. To be sure, it does not always get it; but then the alternative punishment is a mediocre life, and in what way is a mediocre life preferable to affliction? Moreover, even in the case of great misfortune such people's lives are probably still mediocre. So far as conjecture is possible about sensibility, it would seem that the evil within a man is a protection against the external evil that attacks him in the form of pain. One must hope so, and that for the impenitent thief God has mercifully reduced to insignificance such useless suffering. In fact, it certainly is so, because that is the great temptation which affliction offers: It is always possible for an afflicted man to suffer less by consenting to become wicked.

The man who has known pure joy, if only for a moment, and who has therefore tasted the flavour of the world's beauty, for it is the same thing, is the only man for whom affliction is something devastating. At the same time, he is the only man who has not deserved this punishment. But, after all, for him it is no punishment; it is God himself holding his hand and pressing it rather hard. For, if he remains constant, what he will discover buried deep under the sound of his own lamentations is the pearl of the silence of God.

(*The Simone Weil Reader*)

NO ONE WOULD EVER MISTAKE Simone Weil's life for a mediocre life. It was by all accounts and in many ways an extraordinary life. By the middle-class standards most of us carry around like a lead weight, it was a singularly crazy life. And for institutional Christians one of the maddest aspects of her life was her persistent refusal to receive Baptism.

As early as 1934 she became increasingly interested in Christianity. Her earlier years had been void of any religious training, but it was with a kind of personal recognition that she began to study or, more importantly, to deepen her appreciation of the Christian Mystery. As her death approached, she was regularly visited by a Roman Catholic priest, but she persisted in believing that Baptism was not possible for her.

Some have romanticized this and suggested, with little evidence, that the suffering of her fellow Jews made her hold back from being received into full communion with the Church. (In 1943 no one outside of a very select number was aware of the dimentions of the Holocaust.) The real answer is probably much more complicated, and one is tempted to link her refusal of food at the end to that other refusal. In some way, a way which reduces the notion of "baptism of desire" to vague insignificance, she was already a Christian.

During the 10 days she spent at Solesmes in

1938, she made the acquaintance of an under-graduate from Oxford who, she says, was a true angel, or messenger, because he introduced her to the 17th-century English metaphysical poets. Settling down to read them with her usual thoroughness, she fixed especially upon George Herbert's "Love." From then on whenever her migraine was at a particularly painful crisis, she would recite the poem to herself, "fixing all my attention on it and clinging with all my soul to the tenderness it enshrines":

> Love bade me welcome; yet my soul drew
>> back,
>> Guilty of dust and sin.
> But quick-eyed Love, observing me grow slack
>> From my first entrance in,
> Drew nearer to me, sweetly questioning
>> If I lack'd anything.
>
> "A guest," I answer'd, "worthy to be here."
>> Love said, "You shall be he."
> "I, the unkind, ungrateful? Ah, my dear,
>> I cannot look on Thee."
> Love took my hand and smiling did reply,
>> "Who made the eyes but I?"
>
> "Truth, Lord; but I have marr'd them: let my
>> shame
>> Go where it doth deserve."

"And know you not," says Love, "Who bore
      the blame?"
      "My dear, then I will serve."
"You must sit down," says Love, "and taste
      my meat."
      So I did sit and eat.

As with the Gregorian chant, she supposed
her attachment to the poem to be aesthetic and
believed that she was reciting it simply as a
beautiful poem. But the recitation had—without
her knowing it—the virtue of a prayer. As she
explained four years later to her friend Father
Perrin, one day while she was reciting the poem,
"Christ himself came down and took possession
of me." In a letter to another friend, she says of
the same experience:

> At a moment of intense physical pain, when I
> was making the effort to love, although be-
> lieving I had no right to give any name to the
> love, I felt, while completely unprepared for
> it (I had never read the mystics), a presence
> more personal, more certain, and more real
> than that of any human being; it was inacces-
> sible both to sense and to imagination, and it
> resembled the love that irradiates the tenderest
> smile of somebody one loves.

She certainly regarded this as the supreme

experience of her life. As a result, the necessity of sacramental Baptism may have been so relativized in her own mind as to make it super-fluous.

BY ORDINARY STANDARDS there is something tragic and incomplete about her life and her death. Raymond Rosenthal expressed it well and consolingly when he said that her special genius "was to show that private suffering can have a vital public social value."

Simone Weil died as a witness to her faith. She proclaimed in her own, sometimes tortured, way that "God loves you now!" She saw herself as "the bell which tolls to bring others to church." As with most great-souled persons, both her life and her death witnessed to the God who loves to the end. And in that sense her life was not tragic by any usual understanding of that term.

Simone Weil lived through a period of great tragedy and great uncertainty in our history. Perhaps only in such a life as hers, a life in which much was unresolved and still more was uncertain, could the silent love of God for his creation be announced.

At the end of *The Cocktail Party*, after Celia's martyrdom has been described to her friends ("It would seem that she must have been crucified very near an ant-hill"), her *directeur,* the psychiatrist Harcourt-Reilly, explains why his own face showed no surprise or horror at the news of her terrible death. It serves perhaps as a partial explanation of the strange, hardly to be emulated and yet somehow appropriate, end of the short life of Simone Weil.

—When I first met Miss Coplestone, in this room,
I saw the image, standing behind her chair,
Of a Celia Coplestone whose face showed the astonishment
Of the first five minutes after a violent death.
If this strains your credulity, Mrs. Chamberlayne,
I ask you only to entertain the suggestion
That a sudden intuition, in certain minds,
May tend to express itself at once in a picture.
This happens to me, sometimes. So it was obvious
That here was a woman under sentence of death.
That was her destiny. The only question
Then was, what sort of death? I could not know;
Because it was for her to choose the way of life
To lead to death, and, without knowing the end

Yet choose the form of death. We know the
     death she chose.
I did not know that she would die in this way,
She did not know. So all that I could do
Was to direct her in the way of preparation.
That way, which she accepted, led to this
     death.
And if that is not a happy death, what death
     is happy?

THEOLOGIA:

DOROTHY L. SAYERS
AND THE GREAT MYSTERY STORY

FOR MOST OF US the word *mystery* evokes associations with Erle Stanley Gardner's Perry Mason, Agatha Christie's Miss Marple, or Dorothy L. Sayers' Lord Peter Wimsey. But Miss Sayers concerned herself with far more fundamental questions than the mystery buff's conventional "who done it?" In her theological writings, she pursued the ultimate "who done it?"—that is, "who made the world and all that therein is?"

Let us return to that scrap of paper tacked to a Tuscan pulpit, *"Ora, Dio ti ama!"* ("God loves you now!"). A question naturally arises, whether we put it into words or ask it in our heart: How do I know this to be so? Whether we like it or not, we find ourselves engaged in a theological debate.

Theology is wrongly taken to be the particular preserve of specialists, people who make a profession out of sometimes extremely obscure mutterings about God and humanity. To be human, however, means to be a questing and questioning being; we might even say of ourselves that we are animals who ask questions. And such questioning is not to be considered a fault but rather one of our glories as creatures who bear within our intellects, imaginations and wills God's image. Theology is an exercise of that glory. Anselm of Canterbury once defined theology as *"fides quaerens intellectum"* ("faith seeking understanding").

The Christian faith is faith in the mystery of God, but it is not irrational or absurd, as some outsiders and even some Christians think it to be. The preeminent Roman Catholic theologian of our time, Father Karl Rahner, on the occasion of his 75th birthday, put it well when asked to identify the center of his theology:

. . . [T]hat can't be anything else but God as mystery and Jesus Christ, the crucified and risen One, as the historical event in which this God turns irreversibly towards us in self-communication. . . .

We have to remember that humanity is unconditionally directed toward God, a God which we ourselves are not. And yet, with this God, who in every respect infinitely surpasses us, with this God Himself, we do have *something to do*; God is indeed not only the *absolutely distant One*, but the *absolutely near One*, absolutely near, also, in His history.

It is because God has disclosed himself to us, is near to us, that we have something to do with him. Callow unbelief and false piety alike would dissuade us from thinking about God, but to be fully human demands thinking—sometimes hard thinking—about God. Rahner went on to say that humanity is not so much directed toward what it can control in knowledge as toward the absolute mystery. But,

. . . that mystery is not just an unfortunate remainder of what is not yet known but rather the blessed goal of *knowledge* which comes to itself when it is with the incomprehensible One, and not in any other way.

Theology, then, is the act of articulating in the most coherent language possible what we believe and why we believe *here and now*. Theology is not done in some timeless, spaceless, ahistorical realm, but in the midst of life's folly and grandeur, virtue and viciousness, wisdom and ignorance. Some among us who are specially gifted add the dimension of imagination to this enterprise.

Every *believing* Christian is also meant to be—insofar as this is possible "according to our diverse estates"—an *inquiring* Christian prepared to express, *at least for oneself*, the reasons for the faith he or she has within. Thus every Christian is called to *do* theology. Few of her academic contemporaries surpassed Dorothy L. Sayers in the doing of theology, and so we turn now to her as an exemplar of the Christian questioner each of us is meant in our own way to be.

ONE OF THE RECENT BIOGRAPHIES of Dorothy L. Sayers is entitled very appropriately *Such a Strange Lady,* for strange she was. Born in 1893, the daughter of a country clergyman in Huntingdonshire, she was given an excellent education first at home, then at Somerville College, Oxford (later fictionalized in her book *Gaudy Night*), where she took first-class honors in French. After a not very successful interval of teaching, she finally landed in London. There she took a job with an advertising firm, conducting what were then regarded as extremely successful sales campaigns for such items as Coleman's mustard! At the same time she began writing her delightful series of detective stories, creating the engaging Lord Peter Wimsey as her chief protagonist, although she is remembered by aficionados for other characters as well.

Unhappy in her first love affair, she met in 1923 the man who was to change her life—or, rather, to prevent her from changing it and keep her tied to her job in advertising for another eight years. It is not known whether he was a "grand passion," just a casual acquaintance, or someone taken up for the "experience" supposed to be so necessary for the writer. Whatever the motive, Dorothy realized by June, 1923, that she was pregnant. Typically, she was profoundly shocked at herself, returned to her parents' home and was delivered of a son in January, 1924.

One of the mysteries of Dorothy L. Sayer's life is her subsequent treatment of her illegitimate child. She gave him over to an eccentric cousin to raise, but she took no steps to conceal his identity as her child; nor would she consent to place him for adoption. Yet she seems never to have mentioned him, not even in conversation with her closest friends, although she provided amply for his upbringing and education.

In 1926 she did finally marry an ex-soldier, Oswald Fleming, with whom she maintained a not very happy but loyal relationship until his death in 1950. He appears to have been a kind of "professional" ex-army officer, indolent, semi-alcoholic, glad to permit his wife's considerable royalties to provide him with bed and board and pint.

In the 1930's Dorothy's interests moved away from popular fiction, at which she had proved herself so adept, to explicitly religious subjects. Raised as a devout Christian by her parents whom she dearly loved, she had undergone a conventional youthful rebellion against institutional religion, declaring to her tutor at Oxford that she considered herself an agnostic. But this seems to have been mere pose; even in her earliest detective novels there is evidence of a profound Christian intellect at work.

In the 30's she wrote a number of verse plays in the genre of her friends Charles Williams and T.S. Eliot, whom she joined in contributing to the annual festival sponsored by the Friends of Canterbury Cathedral. Her play-writing culminated in 1941 with her remarkable radio drama about Jesus, *The Man Born to Be King*. This highly controversial work—she was so bold as to give cockney accents to some of the disciples—was perhaps the forerunner of *Godspell* and *Jesus Christ, Superstar*. It is a highly readable script even today, written by an author committed to making the gospel contemporary and possessed of the kind of poetic imagination necessary to the task.

It is interesting to read the arguments of those who attempted to pressure the BBC (British Broadcasting Corporation) into canceling the broadcasts. Chief among them was the Council of the Lord's Day Observance Society. This group felt that to suggest that Jesus and his disciples did not speak in the elegant tones of the King James Bible would diminish ordinary folks' respect for Holy Writ.

Broadcasts, lecturing, yet more writing—all put Dorothy L. Sayers' name before the public as more than just the author of an extraordinarily popular series of detective novels. During the 40's and 50's, although not formally associated with the Inklings, that unique circle of theologues and Oxford intellectuals centered around the poet and novelist Charles Williams, she knew and sympathized with many of them: C.S. Lewis, Owen Barfield, J.R.R. Tolkien and the Londoner T.S. Eliot. At the time of her sudden death in 1957,

Dorothy L. Sayers was regarded as one of the most effective apologists for orthodox Christianity in this century.

Even today, partly as a result of the successful adaptation of the Wimsey novels for TV, nearly all of her books—the stories, the translations, the theological works—have a ready audience. A number of studies of Dorothy L. Sayers' life and work are in preparation. She may shortly assume something of the proportion of what is called "the C.S. Lewis industry."

WHAT WAS THE SECRET of this "strange lady's" ability to communicate the power and the splendor of the gospel, not simply to intellectuals but to ordinary readers? To my mind she had the gift of making the Christian mysteries more exciting than detective thrillers. Christian theology was for her a hair-raising adventure which gives human life a creative edge. The problem to her mind was that generations of earnest Christians had rendered the gospel innocuous. Thus she could write in *The Man Born to Be King:*

> Not Herod, not Caiaphas, not Pilate, not Judas ever contrived to fasten upon Jesus Christ the reproach of insipidity; that final indignity was left for pious hands to inflict. To make of His story something that could

neither startle, nor shock, nor terrify, nor excite, nor inspire a living soul is to crucify the Son of God afresh and put Him to an open shame.

Dorothy once described herself as "engaged in my diabolical occupation of going to and fro in the world and walking up and down in it." She delighted in tweaking the noses of solemn believers in modernity as well as shocking the respectably pious. But hers was more than a virtuoso exercise in debunking contemporary dogmas and waking up the slumbering Church. She was appalled at what she perceived to be the sheer ignorance of nominal Christians about the creeds in which they professed belief.

Even harder to fathom was the arrogant misunderstanding of those who rejected what they mistakenly believed to be Christianity. As she wrote in her 1949 book *Creed or Chaos*:

It would not perhaps be altogether surprising if, in this nominally Christian country, where the Creeds are daily recited, there were a number of people who knew all about Christian doctrine and disliked it. It is more startling to discover how many people there are who heartily dislike and despise Christianity without having the faintest notion what it is. If you tell them, they cannot believe you. I do not mean that they cannot believe the doctrine: that would be understandable enough, since it takes some believing. I mean that they simply cannot believe that anything so interesting, so exciting, and so dramatic can be the orthodox Creed of the Church.

That was of course her distinctive gift, to make Christian teaching—or as she preferred, mincing no words, "Christian dogma"—interesting, exciting and dramatic.

HER OWN HIGHLY IMAGINATIVE bent helped to make her theological work a vivid restatement of traditional Christian teaching. Indeed, it is her powerful literary and poetic imagination which lends to her religious writing such a bracing freshness. In her essay "Towards a Christian Aesthetic," she drops some clues for us about the role of the imagination, "the image-making faculty," in the business of theology. If, as she argues, we commit ourselves to saying that the Christian revelation uncovers for us the nature of *all* truth, then it must disclose to us the nature of that truth which is imagination's child, art itself.

In her view the chief reason it has been possible for Christian devotees to reduce the gospel to insipid sentimentality is that we have failed to hammer out a truly Christian aesthetic, that is, a

Christian philosophy of the imagination. We have, therefore, only reluctantly granted the imagination admission to the theological enterprise.

Our problem is Plato. We have inherited his strictures against the kinds of art he wished banished from the perfect state. His whole handling of the thing strikes us today as strange and contradictory, and yet his aesthetic has dominated all our critical thinking for many centuries, and has influenced the attitude of the Church more than the Church knows.

In the 10th book of the *Republic,* Plato decides to banish all representation of every kind (drama, painting, sculpture, poetry) for two reasons. The first is that imitation is a kind of cheating. As Dorothy L. Sayers remarks, Plato saw representational art as merely an imitation of an imitation, "a deceptive trick which tickles and entertains while turning men's mind away from the contemplation of the eternal realities." Plato's second reason for banishing all representational art— even when what is represented is in itself good and noble—is that the effect on the audience is bad, leading them to dissipate the emotions and energies that ought to be used for tackling the problems of life.

In the jargon of modern psychology, Plato is saying that art of this kind leads to fantasy and daydreaming. Aristotle, 50 years later, defended it because such entertainment helps people blow off steam. Who was right?

Dorothy L. Sayers argues that they are both dead wrong, even though they were both correctly concerned with the moral effect of art. The true work of imagination is something *new*—not the copy or representation of anything. Something has been *created*. This word—the idea of art as *creation*—is the one important contribution Christianity has to make to aesthetics.

Unhappily we use the word *creation* very sloppily indeed: This new hat is a "creation!" And we do this because we do not relate the notion properly to theology.

Dorothy L. Sayers regards it as significant that the Greeks did not have the concept of "creation" in their aesthetic at all. They looked on a work of imagination as a kind of *techne,* a manufacture. And because their theology lacked the concept of creation, they could not look on history the way the Jews did, as the continual act of God fulfilling himself in creation.

WHAT DOES IT MEAN to say that God creates? And how does his act compare with the artist's act of creation?

We begin by saying that God created the universe "out of nothing"—bound by no conditions of any kind. With this there can be no human comparison: The human artist is *in* the universe and bound by its conditions. He can create only within that framework and out of the material supplied by the universe.

But there is a real analogy between the creative act of God and the creative act of the imaginative artist. Sayers explains its basis in the way Christian theology teaches that God creates:

> Christian theology replies that God, who is Trinity, creates by or through His Second Person, His Word or Son, who is continually begotten from the First Person, the Father, in an eternal creative activity. And certain theologians have added this very significant comment: *the Father*, they say, *is only known to Himself by beholding His image in His Son.*

Here Sayers acknowledges that a new word has crept into her argument by way of theology, the word *image*. Suppose, having rejected the words *copy, imitation* and *representation* as inadequate, we substitute the word *image*. Suppose we say that what the artist is doing is to *image forth* something or other, and connect that with the phrase in Hebrews which describes God's Son as "the brightness of his glory and the *express image* of his person" (Heb 1:3, KJV, emphasis added). The artist, then, by the use of imagination "creates" in a way analogous to God.

Of course, she says:

> There is something which is, in the deepest
> sense of the words, *unimaginable*, known to
> Itself (and still more, to us) only by the image
> in which it expresses Itself through creation.
> Christian theology teaches very emphatically
> that the Son, who is the express image, is not
> the copy, or imitation, or representation of the
> Father, nor yet inferior or subsequent to the
> Father in any way. The depths of their myste-
> rious being, the unimaginable and the image,
> are finally one and the same.

This, for Dorothy L. Sayers, gives us a clue to
the real artist's task, and to the imaginative
theologian's as well. The artist/theologian is
simply a person like ourselves, but with an
exceptional power of revealing his or her experience by expressing it so that we *recognize* the
experience as our own. Therefore the greatest
artists and the greatest theologians have much in
common: They both deal in recognition.

Dorothy L. Sayers stresses the word *recognize*.
By thus recognizing his experience in its expression, the artist makes it his own—integrates it into
himself. It is no longer something happening *to*
him; it is something happening *in* him. Thus the
act of artistic creation is threefold—a trinity of
experience, expression and recognition. Such a

way of looking at the artist's task comes very close to describing the theologian's enterprise as well.

What artists (or theologians) do for themselves, they can also do for us. Since they are human beings like the rest of us, we might reasonably expect that our experience will have something in common with theirs. As Sayers says:

> In the image of *his* expereince, we can *recognize* the image of some experience of our own—something that had happened to us, but which we had never formulated and expressed to ourselves, and therefore never known as a real experience. When we read the poem, or see the play or picture or hear the music, it is as though a light were turned on inside us. We say: "Ah! I recognize that! That is something which I obscurely felt to be going on in and about me, but I didn't know what it was and couldn't express it. But now that the artist has made its image—imaged it forth—for me, I can possess and take hold of it and make it my own and turn it into a source of knowledge and strength."

The Jews, Sayers notes, were forbidden to make any image for worship, because before the revelation of the three-fold unity in which Image and Unimaginable are one, it was too fatally easy to substitute the idol for the Image. But, she concludes:

The Christian revelation set free all the images, by showing that the true Image subsisted within the Godhead Itself—it was neither copy, nor imitation, nor representation, nor inferior, nor subsequent, but the brightness of the glory and the express image of the Person—the very mirror in which reality knows itself and communicates itself in power . . . .

And she ends this essay on a personal and pastoral note:

The great thing, I am sure, is not to be nervous about God—not to try and shut out the Lord Immanuel from any sphere of truth. Art is not He—we must not substitute Art for God; yet this also is He, for it is one of His Images and therefore reveals His nature. Here we see in a mirror darkly—we behold only the images; elsewhere we shall see face to face, in the place where Image and Reality are one.

Although she does not refer to herself explicitly as an artist or poet or even as a theologian in the passages quoted, it is precisely this sort of recognition she so often awakens in her readers. Out of the fabric of her own experience as an occasionally very faltering Christian she managed to weave a sometimes fragmented but richly imaginative tapestry retelling the Christian story. Hers was a faith always seeking understanding:

> The people who hanged Christ never, to do them justice, accused Him of being a bore— on the contrary; they thought Him too dynamic to be safe. It has been left for later generations to muffle up that shattering personality and to surround him with an atmosphere of tedium. We have very efficiently pared the claws of the Lion Judah, certified Him "meek and mild," and recommended Him as a fitting household pet for pale curates and pious old ladies. To those who knew Him, however, He in no way suggested a milk-and-water person; *they* objected to him as a dangerous firebrand. True, He was tender to the unfortunate, patient with honest inquirers, and humble before Heaven; but He insulted respectable clergymen by calling them hypocrites; He referred to King Herod as "that fox"; He went to parties in disreputable company and was looked upon as a "gluttonous man and a wine-bibber, a friend of publicans and sinners"; He assaulted indignant tradesmen and threw them and their belongings out of the Temple; He drove a coach-and-horses through a number of sacrosanct and hoary regulations; He cured diseases by any means that came handy, with a shocking casualness in the matter of other people's

pigs and property; He showed no proper deference for wealth or social position; when confronted with neat dialectical traps, He displayed a paradoxical humor that affronted serious-minded people, and He retorted by asking disagreeably searching questions that could not be answered by rule of thumb. He was emphatically not a dull man in His human lifetime, and if He was God, there can be nothing dull about God either. But He had "a daily beauty in His life that made us ugly," and officialdom felt that the established order of things would be more secure without Him. So they did away with God in the name of peace and quietness.

(*The Man Born to be King*)

A SCHOOLBOY ONCE WROTE in an essay which she delighted to quote on herself, "Then there was Miss Dorothy L. Sayers who turned from a life of crime to join the Church of England." There is a sense in which she did indeed move from the detection of fictional mysteries to the investigation of the Great Mystery Story. She was herself a consummate craftsman and truly believed that "a loose and sentimental theology begets loose and sentimental art-forms." Of neither looseness nor sentimentality can she be accused, not in her mystery stories nor in her theology.

It is not easy for most of us to identify with "the strange lady" who was Dorothy L. Sayers. But her commitment to *theologia,* thinking about God and seeking to express the results of that reflection practically in her own life and for others, links her to those of us not blessed with her strange genius. Without exception each of us has been gifted with intellect and imagination which we are charged to use not only in the humble daily round, but also in our questioning and affirming of the highest and deepest of realities, the mystery of God.

That Mystery Story looms before us as it did for Dorothy L. Sayers. No one is excused from tracing its clues and moving toward the moment of illumination when each of us can exclaim: "I've got it! I know who did it!"

What would Dorothy have made of that bit of brown paper pinned to the pulpit in Tuscany? "God loves you now!" She would have liked its brief and jarring note; after all, she rejoiced in jolting the unwary passersby who had either forgotten (or, more likely, never learned) simple gospel truth. For her that plain placard would have served as the clincher in the trail of clues leading to the solution of the Mystery of which she was so devoted a detective.

LEITURGIA:

EVELYN UNDERHILL
AND THE PIETY
OF WORSHIP

THERE IS NO BETTER WAY to comprehend the sacramental nature of the world than to examine the Christian's role in the world under the concept of *leiturgia*, "worship." It is the quality of worshipfulness which characterizes—or at least ought to characterize—our life in the world. The ultimate reality, what we haltingly and with stumbling words call God, discloses itself not in some higher knowledge or mystical intuition but in and through the world itself, through the people and events and encounters which make up our individual and our corporate lives. In the attempt to make the concept of worship concrete we turn to yet another remarkable woman, Evelyn Underhill.

Evelyn Underhill's name is not a household word, although her two books, *Worship* and *Mysticism*, have seldom if ever gone out of print and continue to be read as classics of the spiritual life. Her interests ranged from the occult to so-called psychic phenomena. Most important to us was her conviction that Christians who differ profoundly on the level of belief may nonetheless be able to worship together. For her, worship was what mattered more than all else.

At All Saints' some years ago I found myself at the House of Retreat in Pleshey, a village in Essex and in the Diocese of Chelmsford. I had been invited to conduct an ecumenical retreat for Roman Catholics and Anglicans in the very place Evelyn Underhill had conducted her famous retreats. I quickly discovered something of the *genius loci*, why it was that Evelyn Underhill so loved the place and chose it for her own remarkable ministry.

The House itself, with its almost perfect chapel, is on the site of a medieval castle surrounded by a moat and extensive, beautifully planted gardens. It was a particularly lovely autumn that year, full of "mists and mellow fruitfulness." Staying at Pleshey in that subdued and quiet season of the year reminded me that one of Evelyn Underhill's favorite poems was Gerard Manley Hopkins' "God's Grandeur," which expresses in incomparable language her hard-won, deeply-held conviction that creation is sacramental.

> The world is charged with the grandeur of God.
> > It will flame out, like shining from shook foil;
> > It gathers to a greatness, like the ooze of oil
> Crushed. Why do men then now not reck his rod?
>
> Generations have trod, have trod, have trod;
> > And all is seared with trade, bleared,
> > > smeared with toil;
> > And wears man's smudge and shares
> > > man's smell: the soil
> Is bare now, nor can foot feel, being shod.
>
> And for all this, nature is never spent;
> > There lives the dearest freshness deep
> > > down things;
> And though the last lights off the black West went
> > Oh, morning, at the brown brink east-
> > > ward, springs—

Because the Holy Ghost over the bent
     World broods with warm breast and with ah!
          bright wings.

If the brown paper tacked to the Tuscan pulpit means anything at all, the fact that God loves
me now signifies just that: Not in some distant
realm above and beyond the dirt and turmoil of
this lovely and terrible world, but *here and now*
"lives the dearest freshness deep down things."
Pleshey vividly reminded me that creation is
God's sacrament.

EVELYN UNDERHILL'S CONVICTION about
the sacramental character of creation was hard-
won, especially if one takes into account her
background. Born in 1875, she was a much-loved
and only child. Shortly after her birth her parents
moved to London, where Evelyn was educated
for the most part at home. Early on she showed a
gift for writing. The Underhills enjoyed both
travel and sailing and shared their enthusiasm
with Evelyn. Even after her marriage in 1907, she
continued to spend an annual holiday with her
mother in Italy.

Baptized and confirmed in the Church of
England, she left that communion impatiently as
a young woman. By the age of 23 she was committed to what she called "the mystic quest" and

had become a young participant in various esoteric societies. Her most recent biographer, Christopher J.R. Armstrong, well describes the Edwardian religious climate she imbibed:

> There was an enormous excitement impalpably everywhere in the air in those days, mysteriously compounded of the psychic, the psychological, the occult, the mystical, the medieval, the advance of science, the self-unfolding of the Absolute, the apotheosis of Art, the rediscovery of the feminine and infatuation simultaneously with both the most unashamedly sensuous and the most ethereally "spiritual." It was indeed the age of the "the soul," one of those periods when a sudden easing of social taboos brings on, or is brought on by, a great sense of personal emancipation and a desire for an El Dorado apparently cold-shouldered and despised by an older, more morose and insensitive generation.

Evelyn Underhill was very much a part of that milieu. Her initiation into an occult group called the Golden Dawn was a natural outcome of her own mystical disposition. In the first decade of the new century she published a series of novels in which the more extreme forms of occultism served as a major theme. It was as a novelist and a poet that she first revealed the direct honesty of thought and steady insight with which, under the guidance of Baron Friedrich von Hügel, she later illuminated the mystical way for so many readers and pilgrims.

Evelyn Underhill did not have to write or, indeed, do anything in particular. Without reproach she might have become a purely domestic figure administering a household, carrying out her social obligations and pursuing a life of prayer and a little self-gratifying research. It was her choice to work, and she did not do things by halves. Looking after a husband and running the house in Campden Hill Square, entertaining and being entertained, reading, research and writing, worship, prayer and meditation, visiting in poor neighborhoods, holidays away from home, care of her parents—all these found a place in her schedule. Her fundamental axiom was that *all* life was sacred. That—as she would have breezily said in later life—is what the Incarnation is about.

But early in her life the privileges of her class did indeed tempt her to a more rarified interpretation of reality. It is a paradox that the more secure we are materially and temporally, the more apt we are to succumb to the Neoplatonic snare of undervaluing this world and seeking escape from it by way of a "higher illumination." Thus the young people in our own culture most drawn to esoteric religious experience, transcendental meditation and such are not the victims of economic oppression in the ghetto—people who might quite excusably seek to escape grim reality (as, alas, all too many do through drink and drugs). Rather they are the privileged children of the suburbs, those who—like Evelyn Underhill before them—need not trouble themselves over the nasty necessities of survival.

The spiritual aristocrats who interpret the world as *maya,* illusion, are almost always drawn from the economically advantaged. Gautama Buddha was not the son of a carpenter, but of a king; Siddhartha was not born in a stable, but in a palace.

SOCIOLOGIST OF RELIGION Robert Bellah argues that there are fundamentally two kinds of religion, the religion of the sky father and the religion of the earth mother. The sky religions emphasize the paternal and hierarchical, the legalistic and ascetic aspects of existence. The earth religions, however, emphasize the maternal and communal, the expressive and joyful. Prophecy and high mysticism are the result of the sky religion at its most profound; cosmic harmony and domestic graciousness are the finest outcome of the earth religion. Put into theological language, these two types of religion reflect the reality of God as both transcendent and immanent.

But, as Bellah remarks, either carried to an extreme can have fatal results: The religion of the sky father can become rigid and dogmatic, an escape from personal responsibility; the religion of the earth mother can become a wallowing in the seaminess of this flawed world.

In a brilliant essay entitled "Liturgy and Experience" Bellah writes of the tensions between these two basic types—sky father and earth mother:

> . . . The being-at-home so characteristic of the earth religions becomes an image not of life but of stagnation and death, and the sky father who calls one to leave home is the liberator. Moses was called to leave Egypt and led his people to a new and more precarious home. He spent his days in wandering and died in the wilderness. Jesus too was a wanderer. "The birds of the air have their nests, and the foxes of the field their holes; but the son of man has not where to lay his head" (Mt 8:20). Buddha declared the world to be a burning house and called on his followers to take to the road with only a begging bowl in hand. In Japan, to become a monk is to *shukke,* to leave home. In all these cases there is a home,

but it is a sky home, Kingdom of Heaven, Western Paradise. The tension between this earth and the sky home generates unease, and often pressure for social change, for the greater realization of values in human society. This is the significance of prophetic religion, the achievements of which we forget at our peril when we reject the modern world too radically.

Although she never expressed it in this way, there can be no doubt that Evelyn Underhill felt just such a tension in her own life. And this same tension is felt especially in American culture today.

Robert Bellah suggests—and here he is at variance with the mainstream of the Judeo-Christian tradition—that this tension between sky and earth religion can be resolved by what he calls the experience of nothingness. In this experience, he argues, we find that the bottom has dropped out. In the depth of the earth-home and the sky-home, there is no home at all; in the root of every belief, there is an absolute doubt; at the core of every self and every culture, there is absolute nothingness.

Such a radical and shattering experience is not ultimately, however, an experience of despair. Bellah argues that the powerful element of death in it is overcome by the possibility of rebirth. The experience of nothingness exposes humanity in some deep and unconscious way as the creator of its own myths: a frightening, but also an immensely liberating experience.

The experience of nothingness is, of course, not new in human history. Evelyn Underhill traced it masterfully in her book *Mysticism*—and then began the process of her own rebirth under the tutelage of the man who became her spiritual director, Baron Friedrich von Hügel. The fruit of this process was her first, hard-won conviction that all of reality was sacramental—a conviction born of intense struggle.

Von Hügel wrote of this struggle in his masterpiece, *The Mystical Element in Religion.* He remarks on the inherent danger when an individual, independently of any "concrete, social, and devotional helps and duties," develops a taste for the contemplative life. Mere mysticism can be dangerous and even destructive without the ordinary responsibilities and commitments of daily life. Membership in a family, a nation and a Church provides both a framework for and a check upon the mystical tendency.

That Evelyn Underhill was just such an "abstractive soul" there can be little doubt. Before she came directly under von Hügel's tutelage, she came close—as she later realized—to the soul "in danger" as he described it.

His remedy for her and for others like her was to urge upon her what he called a "Catholic" approach: He led her to acknowledge her creatureliness, to accept the economy of redemption as something proportioned to the human scale, not requiring one to abandon humanity, but to seek and find him in others, in the Church and the world.

Von Hügel reveals a clear understanding that the besetting temptation of the person endowed with a mystical temperament is to emigrate from the mundane world, to escape into the "desert," to scale the heights where the rarified air is too thin for mere mortals to breathe. It was Evelyn Underhill's triumph that her life, if anything, was not a flight from the world but a deepening involvement in and commitment to the world, a triumph built on her mentor's advice.

A major aspect of the practical program von Hügel outlined for Evelyn in his letters was his wish that she involve herself more deeply in the lives of the poor, especially through the discipline of visiting them in their homes. He believed—and rightly—that such a practice would strengthen Evelyn Underhill in the struggle against her inner tendency toward angelism (an excessive supernaturalism) and lead her toward a sacramental piety.

BESIDES *MYSTICISM*, which continues to this day to be her most popular work, it is significant that Underhill's other major book is entitled *Worship*. For her life's pilgrimage was indeed a movement from an intensely introspective and subjective personal piety to a more corporate and Eucharistic piety—in other words, from mysticism to worship.

What seems clear is that the direction of her religious history was away from esoteric dabbling in mystical phenomena and toward a committed sacramental devotion. She discovered that it was not through Ouija boards and tarot cards that the divine might be felt and experienced, but through the simplest of human gestures: cleansing water poured, bread and wine shared, reconciling words spoken.

She had known well from early in her life of the importance of ritual and routine in one's life, not least in one's religious life. A character in one of her early novels goes up to Oxford where "the ingenious aberrations of modern theology had already effaced the imprint of an intense and tractarian past." Here he falls out with orthodox Christianity and suffers a period of agnosticism described by his college tutor as a typical instance of "little attacks of intellectual measles." Of the young doubter's attraction to the secret society of the Masons, Evelyn Underhill remarks: "Your dreamer may do without a creed, but he always wants a ritual. . . ."

It is said of Evelyn Underhill that she attached enormous significance to even the simplest of religious rituals, taking infinite pains to see that the liturgy at Pleshey, for example, was beautifully and sensitively rendered. It was not mere aestheticism which moved her to set such importance upon liturgical ceremony; rather, by the time she finally committed herself to remaining a communicant in the Church of England, she was fully convinced that through the gestures of the dance of the liturgy God discloses his reality to us. She quotes her beloved teacher, von Hügel, in *Worship*:

> I cannot in thinking it over find other than two great principles and facts. . . .There is the *sacramental principle,* the waking up of spirit under the stimulus of sense, and this comes, I take it, simply from our soul-and-body compoundness. And then there is the *principle of the community,* of sharing our religion, and of getting it deep and tender through sharing it, with every kind of educated, semi-educated and uneducated fellow-believer.

Christian worship, because of its incarnational character, is always directed towards the sanctification of life. All worship has a creative aim, for it is a movement of the creature in the direction of Reality. God uses the simple gifts of creation as the means whereby his presence is made real, for beneath all the ceremonial of the Church's sacraments are starkly elemental deeds and words. Evelyn Underhill believed that the Christian is required to use "the whole of his existence as sacrament material."

She returned often to historic Christianity's conviction that somehow everything human can be offered and consecrated to God, thereby contributing to the divine glory. As she writes in *Worship*:

> Historical Christianity, with its appointed prayers for each period of the day and night, its blessings of every meal and every activity, its solemn consecrations of birth and marriage, its rites for the restoring of the sinful and the sanctifying of sickness and death, its loving care for the departed, following the rhythm of human existence from its beginning to its apparent end and beyond, has always shown itself sharply aware of this.

With maturity, she came to embrace fully Archbishop William Temple's contention that Christianity is the most materialistic of the world religions. But the seductive escapism of a pseudo-Christian gnosticism and the anguish of agnostic doubt continued to trouble her even into her later years. Two hostile currents existed in Evelyn Underhill: the purely mystical and philosophical, and the Catholic incarnational. Only at the end of her life did she seem to have succeeded in transforming the former into the latter.

WE WOULD SERIOUSLY MISINTERPRET her life, however, if we supposed that Evelyn Underhill was a kind of recluse, living always on a high mystical plane. She had an unusually happy marriage, marred only by its childlessness, and she belonged to a sociable circle of novelists and writers. Like many women of her class, she spent a certain amount of time in "doing good," visiting in the homes of the poor. But, unlike her peers who assumed all too easily the patronizing air of Lady Bountiful, she seems to have become friends with many of the poor whom she visited.

She was a faithful correspondent with friends of all kinds, whether in letters of spiritual advice or in delightful descriptions of people and places. Her selected letters have been edited by her friend Charles Williams and are valuable both for their spiritual insight and because she was a most engaging storyteller. The homeliness and the lively humor of her life shines in her writing as it shone in her speaking.

She had a rare gift, perhaps because of her

own rather unusual religious history, for winning the confidence of those who could not relate their religious experience to the institutional Church. She appears in the memoirs of others as a delightful friend, imaginative in human everyday relations, easy to talk to and always ready to meet new people.

Her friendship with the brilliant if erratic Monsignor Robert Hugh Benson influenced the growth in Evelyn of a strong attraction to the Catholic Church. But by 1923 she was secure in her decision to remain a communicant in the Church of England. Some of her Roman Catholic friends, however, would continue to urge her to be "received."

It is difficult to recapture the atmosphere then prevailing in England and to a lesser extent in the United States in which many Anglicans were experiencing what was called "Roman fever." Evelyn Underhill was not exempt from occasional bouts. In a letter to her friend Dom John Chapman, the Abbot of Downside, she expressed her position:

> I have been for years now a practicing Anglo-Catholic . . . and solidly believe in the Catholic status of the Anglican Church as to Orders and Sacraments, little as I appreciate many of the things done among us. It seems

to be a respectable suburb of the City of God—
but all the same part of Greater London. I
appreciate the superior food, etc., to be had
nearer the centre of things. But the whole point
to me is in the fact that the Lord has put me
here, keeps on giving me more and more jobs
to do for souls here, and has never given me
orders to move on. In fact when I have been
inclined to think of this, something has always
stopped me: and if I did it, it would be purely
out of self-interest and self-will. I know what
the push of God is like, and should obey it if it
came—at least I trust and believe so.

Anglican Underhill remained for the rest of
her life. The sacramentalism to which she had
been attracted in the Roman Catholic Church—
the conviction that it is through the material and
sensible (poured water, broken bread, conjugal
love) that God's presence is made real in the
world—was for her available at least implicitly
in the Church of England, especially as a result of
the Oxford Movement and the subsequent
Catholic revival. Church of England she had been,
Church of England she would remain.

TOWARD THE END OF HER LIFE she finally
fixed upon the most obvious Christian doctrine
for the reconciliation of sky religion and earth

religion, of transcendence and immanence: Incarnation of the Logos, the enfleshment in history of the eternal and the divine. Evelyn Underhill saw this—after many years of struggling with the sheer brute contingency of the Rabbi of Nazareth—as the center of her faith.

The mystic is not really comfortable with the transitory and the conditioned, and Evelyn Underhill was no exception. It was a struggle for her to accept into her faith the incarnational principle. She was quick to confess that her natural bent was far from Christocentric. As she once said:

> You see I come to Christ through God, whereas quite obviously lots of people come to God through Christ. But I can't show them how to do that. All I know is the reverse route.

In the end, however, Jesus was the center of her faith, and the motivating force for worship.

> Even were we to set aside the sacred character of its historic origin and its supernatural claim, no other rite could so well embody the homely and transcendental paradox of Christianity; the universal divine action, and the intimate divine approach to every soul; the food of daily life, and the mystery of eternal life, both given at once; the historical memorial perpetually renewed, yet finding its

fulfillment in a real and enduring Presence unfettered by the categories of time and space.

She expressed the centrality the Eucharist had assumed for her most beautifully in her poem "Corpus Christi," written in 1912 at the beginning of her pilgrimage away from esotericism and back to orthodox Christianity:

Yea, I have understood
How all things are one great oblation made:
He on our altars, we on the world's road.
Even as this corn,
Earth-born,
We are snatched from the sod;
Reaped, ground to grist,
Crushed and tormented in the Mills of God,
And offered at Life's hands, a living
    Eucharist.

A snapshot reproduced in Margaret Cropper's biography of Evelyn Underhill speaks volumes. Taken toward the end of her life, probably about 1938 (she died in 1941 at 66), it shows her with W.H. Frere, one of the founders of the Mirfield Fathers and the then retired Bishop of Truro. Bishop Frere has the look of a man who deeply wishes he were somewhere else, his eyes fixed firmly on the middle distance. Next to him, her mouth open in full, upper middle-class gush, sits Evelyn Underhill, having a nice gossip with the old gentleman. Evelyn Underhill became with age a more real and simple person; gone were the bizarre posturings of the Golden Dawn and the feverish rhetoric of *fin-de-siecle* piety.

Perhaps it was no more than the discipline of being with the poor and becoming their friend which revealed to her the holiness of ordinary life; perhaps it was the weekly, sometimes daily, Holy Communion of which she increasingly made herself a part which helped to transform her. Whatever the case, the priest who knew her well wrote after her death:

> It was in the last stage of her spiritual development that she reached the heights for which she had longed, and this was due very largely to the great work of spiritual direction to which God called her. *She found in the care of those sent to her all the tenderness and pastoral anxiety which enabled her to rise above the intellect into a fuller communion with the love of God* [emphasis added].

Evelyn Underhill would have liked that little piece of brown paper tacked to the Tuscan pulpit. "Yes," she would have said firmly, "God does love me now!" and then she would have gone chattily on, "You see, the extraordinary thing is that I used to think he had very bad judgment in doing such a thing, but now I see that he can't help himself."

MOTHER TERESA
AND SOMETHING
BEAUTIFUL FOR GOD

A FEW YEARS AGO Malcolm Muggeridge, our century's Socratic gadfly, was invited to preach one Sunday morning in King's Chapel at Cambridge. The night before, the Dean had a small dinner party to which I was invited to meet Mr. Muggeridge. Our initial conversation went something like this:

> *Dean:* Mr. Muggeridge, this is Father Joseph Goetz, an American Roman Catholic priest.

M.M. (with a saturnine grimace): Roman Catholic! Aha!

Goetz (looking alarmed): How do you do?

M.M.: Aha! Roman Catholic priest!

Goetz (looking toward quickest route for exit and saying with less than perfect honesty): I am pleased to meet you.

M.M. (going for the jugular): Aha! It's your stock-in-trade, Father, isn't it, to keep us all believing?

Goetz (icily calm): No. Faith is a gift of God.

M.M.: Harumph!

Happily, that was not the whole of our conversation; but it did not go well until I mentioned having met Mother Teresa of Calcutta, the woman who provides the focus for this chapter. Then something astonishing and magical happened to the elfin, wrinkled face of Mr. Muggeridge.

Suddenly I was no longer a stranger amid the alien corn, but almost a co-conspirator, someone who—however briefly—shared a wonderful secret.

The secret we shared was a personal impression of the woman whom one writer has described as "an ikon of charity," a symbol of what it means to express Christian love through the service of others. There is therefore a kind of inevitability in turning to Mother Teresa if we would in our time make concrete the concept of *diakonia*, "service."

I hope some inner logic of this book's unfolding has already paved the way for this final chapter on *diakonia*. But even if not, it can still be argued that the concept of diakonia, ministry, expresses as well as any the sum and substance of what it means to be a Christian.

If you believe that God loves you now, then plainly you are meant to express that love in your encounters with others, whom God also loves *now*. And that means that your life for those with whom you live is that of ministry. If the best way to speak of God is that he is "for us," that in the depth of Being itself there is somehow a mysterious and yet utterly real ministry of service to creation (a kenosis, an outpouring), then the same must be true of each of us. It cannot be denied that every baptized Christian is called to ministry, to service.

What would Mother Teresa make of the message on the brown paper tacked to that Tuscan pulpit? It is not easy to envision her on a holiday in Tuscany—it is hard to see her on holiday anywhere (rather like imagining the Queen of England selling Tupperware or the Dalai Lama taking up bowling). But had she been in the

Tuscan church and seen the placard, I have no doubt about her response: "Why, of course. This is just what we are trying to say through our work at our various missions. God loves you now!"

What is there about this simple Yugoslav woman that could make the cynical, world-weary face of Malcolm Muggeridge light up as though illuminated from within? There is no answer to that question in a mere examination of her biography. Indeed, she discouraged any full-blown biographical treatment of her life. She thought of herself (and of other Christians, whether they know it or not) as an instrument of Christ—which meant for her that there was nothing inherently interesting in her life apart from Jesus.

It is true that her life was not very "exciting." She lived as a member of a community and her life was extremely predictable with its daily round of common prayer and work among the poor, both those who came to the centers and those who needed to be visited in their homes, or hovels, or wherever they were to be found.

THE FACTS OF HER LIFE, taken by themselves, are simple enough. She was born of Albanian parents at Skopje, Yugoslavia, one of three children. Educated at the government school, she became a member of the Sodality which was under the spiritual jurisdiction of the Jesuit community. One of the Yugoslav Jesuits who had volunteered to work in the Archdiocese of Calcutta sent home enthusiastic letters describing the Bengal mission field, letters which were read to the young Sodalists. When young Agnes Gouxha Bejaxhui caught his enthusiasm and volunteered for the Bengal Mission, she was encouraged to contact the Sisters of Loretto in Ireland who were also working in Calcutta.

In November, 1928, she was sent to Loretto Abbey near Dublin and from there to India where she began her novitiate at Darjeeling. From 1929 to 1948, the years of Indian self-rule and the horrors of the partition, she taught geography to upper-class Indian girls at St. Mary's High School in Calcutta. For some years she was principal of that school and was also in charge of the Daughters of St. Anne, the Indian religious order attached to the Loretto Sisters. In September, 1946, on what she later called "a day of decision," she requested permission from her superiors to live alone outside the cloister and to work in the Calcutta slums. Her request was taken to Rome and approved.

On August 8, 1948, Mother Teresa laid aside the Loretto habit and clothed herself in a white sari, with blue border and cross on the shoulder. She went to Patna for three months for intensive nursing training with the American Medical Missionary Sisters. By Christmas she was back in Calcutta and living with the Little Sisters of the Poor. That same December she obtained permission to open her first slum school. The following February she moved into a flat in a private house. A month later the first aspirant arrived, a young Bengali girl. In October, 1950, the new congregation of the Missionaries of Charity was approved and instituted in Calcutta, and from there spread throughout India. Thirteen years later the Archbishop of Calcutta blessed the beginnings of a new branch, the Missionary Brothers of Charity.

In 1965 she went to Caracas, Venezuela, to open a center; in 1967, to Ceylon; in 1968, to Tanzania and to Rome as well; in 1969, to Bourke, Australia, to work among the Aborigines; to Melbourne in 1970; to Amman in Jordan in 1970—and so the list continues with new centers added every year to the list. Mother Teresa's decision in 1948 was the catalyst for a worldwide religious movement of service to "the poorest of the poor."

But these "bare bones" of her life story do not adequately explain why that rather odd light suddenly came over the singularly unsentimental face of Malcolm Muggeridge. Or why I felt something of what the Hindus call *darshan*—the gift presence of a holy person—when I met that small Yugoslav woman in the not very appropriate environs of the Cincinnati Cathedral. Her utter simplicity of manner and presence seemed to mock the vulgar gold leaf and black marble which deck the archepiscopal church.

A DISTINGUISHED ECCLESIASTIC relates the story of his introduction to her in Rome some years ago. He and a colleague were to meet with Mother and a few of her sisters just prior to the opening of the Center in one of the worst Roman slums. The bishop's room was done in the rather excessive manner such things tend to be, with imposing, throne-like chairs arranged formally about the walls of the chamber. As Mother and her nuns entered, they greeted the ecclesiastics with reverence and promptly sat themselves down on the marble floor in the usual manner of Hindu peasants. The two churchmen found themselves quite literally looking down on these singular women from high atop their own excessively uncomfortable perchs on the Renaissance chairs. When someone remarked that it must have been a rather awkward moment, the ecclesiastic allowed that a little awkwardness was felt by himself and his colleague, but certainly not by Mother Teresa and her sisters.

The only way that we can hope to understand something of the mystery of this woman is to look at the Gospel of St. John and to behold yet again the visage of that one who is *the* Servant:

> After he had washed their feet, he put his cloak
> back on and reclined at table once more. He
> said to them:
>
>> "Do you understand what I just did for
>>   you?
>> You address me as 'Teacher' and 'Lord,'
>> and fittingly enough,
>> for that is what I am.
>> But if I washed your feet—
>> I who am Teacher and Lord—
>> then you must wash each other's feet."
>>   (John 13:12-14)

In the liturgy for Maundy Thursday, the Mass
of the Lord's Supper, the first reading speaks to
us of the Passover and the rites to be observed as
Israel prepared for the Exodus to the Promised
Land. The second, from Paul's First Letter to the
Corinthians, relays to his converts what he has
heard about the Lord's Last Supper. And the Gospel is that of the Lord's *mandatum.* All three
lessons have strangely recurring words: *pouring
out, handing over, breaking, sharing.* The blood of
the Paschal Lamb is poured upon the doorpost,
its flesh handed over in a ritual meal and then
shared. A cloak is handed over to free the wearer
for his task; water is poured on the dusty feet of

some nondescript fellow-travelers, a slave's ministration shared. Bread is taken, blessed and broken, a cup is poured and handed round.

Pouring out, handing over, breaking, sharing: It is not really surprising that they should be linked, at least in the minds of those who believe. For each is a glimpse—none of them particularly obvious—of what is at the heart of reality. Each of these human gestures of pouring and breaking, handing over and sharing—the blood of a lamb and its roasted flesh, a jug of cleansing water, a loaf of bread, a cup of wine—has its distinctive purpose. And yet they are all part of a pattern, a pattern in which it is possible—as it was for Mother Teresa—to discern the deepest reality of that One whom, with always halting lips, we call the Ground of Being.

It would be surprising were Mother Teresa to have put it in this way. Her writing, which was only occasional and always brief, is not given over to metaphysical reflection. But she would not have denied that these utterly necessary and simple human gestures point beyond themselves to the very nature and personality of God himself.

Take, for example, the gesture of pouring. The most profound thing any of us can say about God in his relation to us is that he has poured existence into his world, into us—those in whom he is imaged. As water is poured from a jug on dusty feet, so has he poured out his own being upon us, bits of clay and sinew.

He has also handed himself over, as food is handed round. He has broken open the gift of life even as bread is broken for the sharing. He has given us to drink deep of his Spirit in the same way one drains a cup of wine for refreshment. Perhaps that is the reason those words are linked in the liturgy for Maundy Thursday: *poured out, handed over, broken, shared.*

If this is truly the nature of God, if the best name we can call him is the Giver of Gifts—the One who pours out, who hands over, breaks open, shares life—what then must be said of us, his children?

In 20 centuries many Christians have answered that question with lives of selfless service, lives of loving ministry. Mother Teresa was only one of them. But think of a Church, a community of Christians who pour out their lives, break their lives for the sharing, hand them over in service. And then ask yourself: is this the way of my life? Is this the Christ-life I gladly proclaim in this widowed and frightened world?

IN MEETING MOTHER TERESA in that gawdy and too expensive cathedral, I felt, in addition to the sense of being in the presence of one of God's dear friends, convicted—not because of anything she said, but because of what she said by her style of life, her presence in the world. And the question, formulated later and battering in my head like a hammer hitting a piece of wood, simply would not go away: Do I pour out my life for others, do I break it in the sharing, do I hand it over in service to others? Most of us can answer that question only very shamefacedly. Subtle are the ways we delude ourselves into believing that we are truly serving others when—in the inner heart which never lies—we know it is ourselves we serve.

If that were all that could be said—that in every martyr there lurks an egoist, in every servant a master, in every priest a prelate—we should despair and confess that our lives are composed of selfishness. But then there looms before us a vision, however dim, of that one whose last night we remember at all times and in all places. We see him laying aside his simple garment and girding himself with a serving apron. He stoops like a slave to pour water on the feet of those who call him Teacher and Lord. And as if this incredible act were not enough to reveal to his followers the shape *their* lives must take and the pattern *they* must assume, after the supper he takes some bread and breaks it—even as his body would be broken in death—and shares a poured cup—even as his blood would be poured out for many. In those simple deeds, simply done, is the assurance not only of a memorial of some past, unforgettable moment. In them, rather, there is an abiding presence, a life which breathes life into us, a power which empowers us, an ordinance which ordains us, a service which makes us servants, an eternal oblation and sacrifice.

That, finally, was Mother Teresa's secret: the abiding presence for her of the Servant of God, Jesus. To see her, as one does, in photographs with the poor, with a dying leper, is to hear yet again the story of the Servant Jesus. And yet it is not the medicine dispensed or the food served or the schooling offered, nor the beds for the dying or the balm for the lepers that gives us a clue to this extraordinary ministry. Mother Teresa has herself declared what is at the heart of all of it:

> In these years of work amongst the people, I have come more and more to realize that it is being unwanted that is the worst disease that any human being can ever experience. Nowadays we have found medicine for TB and consumptives can be cured. For all kinds of diseases there are medicines and cures. But for being unwanted, except there are willing hands to serve and there's a loving heart to love, I don't think this terrible disease can ever be cured.

Because she was deeply aware of the reality of God's love in her own life, she was able to share that love with others. There is nothing mysterious about it, really, as Malcolm Muggeridge would say, unless, of course, you regard love as a mystery.

CONCLUSION

WE HAVE MET SIX WOMEN who, in their various ways, have made concrete some fundamental concepts we share as Christians. Each of the Greek words used to express these concepts denotes an active noun:

Metanoia, the life-long process of conversion, of turning away from sin and turning toward God, is fundamental for any Christian (or, rather, for the would-be Christian).

Koinonia, the challenging task of community-building and community membership—in Teilhard de Chardin's evocative phrase, "building the earth"—flows directly from *metanoia*.

Good news is meant to be shared, and so each is charged to proclaim the *kerygma*, the message of the Cross and the Resurrection.

But because God has gifted even the simplest among us with minds and imaginations, the Christian seeks a deeper understanding of the mystery, hence *theologia*.

Gathered in worship, the community celebrates what it is and what it is becoming through common prayer, *leiturgia*.

The reality of who we are and who our neighbors are, members of the Lord's own body, draws from us the humble ministry of service, *diakonia*.

Six basic Christian realities enfleshed in the lives of six women: Two of these women had babies out of wedlock. One refused Baptism and may have starved herself to death. Another was deeply involved in the occult. Still another was a debutante-aviator. And the last one—well, most of us would find a person who leaves a quiet and worthwhile life to take up her abode with dying lepers in a dying city odd to the point of masochism. Yet, in their own ways, these lives have exemplified to an extraordinary degree the Bishop of Ely's brown paper placard on that Tuscan pulpit.

Each of these women found a way to express within the quite varying confines of their individual commitments—anarchy, feminism, pacifism, worship and prayer, philosophy, marriage, children, scholarship, humble service of the poor—what is really a single, and simple, message: God loves you now.